WI

Baldwinsville,

SEP 0 2 2016

P9-CFV-972

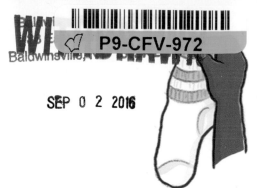

WITHDRAWN
Baldwinsville, NY 13027-2375

written by

Boni Ashburn

illustrated by

Kimberly Gee

the
Class

Beach Lane Books · New York London Toronto Sydney New Delhi

Four are eager, up since dawn.

Three just sit
and yawn
and yawn.

Some are grumpy.

Some keep sleeping.
They don't hear the clock *beep-beep*-ing!

Five begin to look alive.

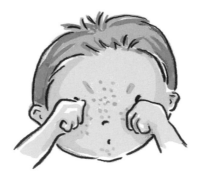

This one's sure he won't survive.

One is tickled.

Two look worried.

One woke late and now she's hurried!

Six
have clothes
laid on
a chair.

Three don't have
a *thing* to wear!

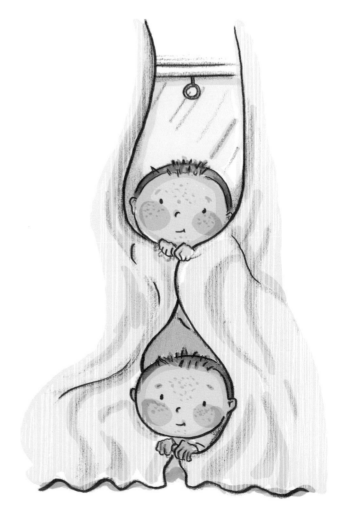

Five
pull on their
favorite
jeans.

Two are
fashionista
queens.

Four wear shirts their mothers chose.

One inspects
her freckled nose.

Ten have bed head.

Nine use combs.

One tries brushes . . .
sprays . . .
and foams . . .

Two put ribbons in their hair.

Four wear day-old underwear.

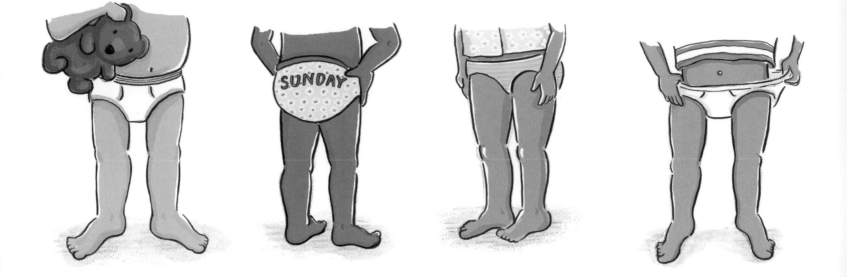

Five can't find a matching sock.

One yells,

"Don't you ever knock?!"

Seven slide on brand-new shoes!

Others have the Old-Shoe Blues.

"Breakfast!" "Hurry!" "Time to eat!"
Shuffling, skipping, running feet . . .

Three have pancakes.

Juice for eight.

Two eat toast.

One drops a plate.

Some have butterflies;
they just nibble.

One's distracted—
dribble . . . dribble.

Three eat cereal from a box.

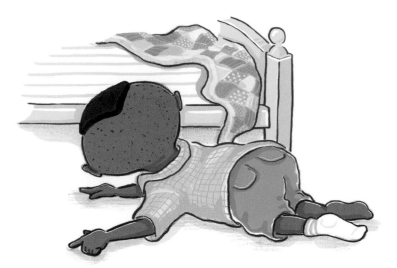

Two keep looking for their socks.

Most brush teeth, but some forget.

Two play games.

One feeds a pet.

Pack up backpacks! Ten have new.
Three get hand-me-downs. One makes do.

Two take snacks and twelve take lunches.

One avoids his sister's punches.

Ready? Set! Time to . . .

GO!

Some move fast!

The rest are sloooooo o o w.

Eight to the bus stop after kisses.

Two run fast—
have near bus-misses!

Four can walk.

Six get a ride.

Three look brave
but teary-eyed.

One trips,
falls,
and skins his knee.

Seven skip in, worry-free.

Over concrete, asphalt, grass,
through the doors, they *all* must pass.

And then . . .

students,

class!

For **Deanna**,
who passed me a note
in class—B. A.

In memory of my grandmother,
Mildred Hobson Gee,
a teacher, librarian, and lover of books—K. G.

 **BEACH LANE BOOKS** • An imprint of Simon & Schuster Children's Publishing Division • 1230 Avenue of the Americas, New York, New York 10020 • Text copyright © 2016 by Boni Ashburn • Illustrations copyright © 2016 by Kimberly Gee • All rights reserved, including the right of reproduction in whole or in part in any form. • BEACH LANE BOOKS is a trademark of Simon & Schuster, Inc. • For information about special discounts for bulk purchases, please contact Simon & Schuster Special Sales at 1-866-506-1949 or business@simonandschuster.com. • The Simon & Schuster Speakers Bureau can bring authors to your live event. For more information or to book an event, contact the Simon & Schuster Speakers Bureau at 1-866-248-3049 or visit our website at www.simonspeakers.com. • Book design by Lauren Rille • The text for this book is set in Archer Book. • The illustrations for this book are rendered in pencil and colored digitally. • Manufactured in China • 0416 SCP • First Edition • 10 9 8 7 6 5 4 3 2 1 • Library of Congress Cataloging-in-Publication Data • Names: Ashburn, Boni, author. | Gee, Kimberly, illustrator. • Title: The class / Boni Ashburn ; illustrated by Kimberly Gee. • Description: First edition. | New York : Beach Lane Books, [2016] | Summary: "Twenty young students, some eager, some nervous, some grumpy, prepare for their very first day of kindergarten"—Provided by publisher. • Identifiers: LCCN 2015029896 | ISBN 978-1-4424-2248-3 (hardback) | ISBN 978-1-4424-4677-9 (eBook) • Subjects: | CYAC: First day of school—Fiction. | Emotions—Fiction. | Stories in rhyme—Fiction. | BISAC: JUVENILE FICTION / School & Education. | JUVENILE FICTION / Social Issues / New Experience. | JUVENILE FICTION / Family / General (see also headings under Social Issues). • Classification: LCC PZ7.A7992 Cl 2016 | DDC [E]—dc23 LC record available at http://lccn.loc.gov/2015029896